tiger tales
an imprint of ME Media, LLC
5 River Road, Suite 128, Wilton, CT 06897
Published in the United States 2013
Originally published in Great Britain 2012
by Hodder Children's Books
a division of Hachette Children's Books
Text copyright © 2012 Rachael Mortimer
Illustrations copyright © 2012 Liz Pichon
CIP data is available
ISBN-13: 978-1-58925-117-5
ISBN-10: 1-58925-117-2
WKT 0612
Printed in China

1 3 5 7 9 10 8 6 4 2

For more insight and activities, visit us at
www.tigertalesbooks.com

FOR FAIRY TALES, FORGOTTEN DINNERS,
AND FOR BEING WHO YOU ARE!
FOR ALL MY FAMILY,
WITH LOTS OF LOVE — R.M.

by Rachael Mortimer

Illustrated by Liz Pichon

RED RIDING HOOD

and the Sweet Little Wolf

tiger tales

ONCE UPON A TIME, there was
a Big Bad Wolf who lived in the woods.
Well, that's not quite true. . . . Really, she was
a Sweet Little Wolf who loved all things
pretty and pink, especially fairy tales.

She lived with her mom and dad who were **very big** and **very bad.**

Mr. and Mrs. Wolf shook their heads.
"When will you ever learn to be a REAL wolf like us?
It's time you went out to get the dinner!"

So Sweet Little Wolf set out.
She hid behind a tree. "I must
be clever and cunning," she
whispered over and over again
as she looked at her mother's list:

DINNER

One onion

Two large potatoes

Three carrots

One sprig of rosemary

One little girl
(tender and juicy)

Just then, Red Riding Hood skipped by on her way
to Grandma's house in the woods.

Sweet Little Wolf couldn't believe her luck!
She scampered slyly and followed her along the path.

Red Riding Hood was
reading a story out loud:

"Once upon a time, with
a flick of a wand, a girl's
rags turned into a beautiful
gown fit for a ball."

It was a fairy tale!
Sweet Little Wolf pricked
up her ears and listened.

Outside Grandma's cottage
Red Riding Hood finished the story:
"**And they lived happily ever after.**"
Then she went inside.

Grandma's House

Gone
to pick
bluebells.
Grandma x

NO
WOLVES

Sweet Little Wolf felt
in her pocket for a handkerchief.
Happy endings always made her cry.
She pulled out her mother's list.

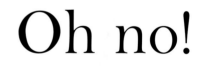

Oh no!

What had
she been doing?
She couldn't go home
without dinner!

Gone to pick bluebells. Grandma ×

There was only one thing to do.
Grandma was out, so Sweet Little Wolf
crept into the cottage after Red Riding Hood.

Grrrrr!
Grrrrr!

She tried her hardest
to make a scary face.
She pointed her sharp claws.
She practiced her best
growl in Grandma's
bedroom mirror. Her
family would be so proud.

But then she spotted a lovely pink robe and
a frilly nightcap on the back of the bedroom door.
Sweet Little Wolf couldn't resist trying them on!

Suddenly, she heard Red Riding Hood in the next room.

The girl was reading again:

"Once upon a time, a girl was rescued from a tower in the middle of a forest by a handsome prince."

Sweet Little Wolf lay down in Grandma's soft, cozy bed.
She would just listen to one more story.

Then she would be a real wolf.

Soon Red Riding Hood heard a strange
noise coming from Grandma's bedroom:

"Snuffle, grunt, snort!
Snuffle, grunt, snort!"

She was surprised. Grandma was supposed to be picking
bluebells in the woods. Why was she snoring in bed?
She looked closer. "Oh, Grandma, what big eyes
you have. And what big teeth!"

Red Riding Hood pulled back the covers and screamed!
It was the Big Bad Wolf!

"Help!" she shouted.
"Wolf!"

A woodcutter heard Red Riding Hood's cry and ran toward the cottage as fast as he could.

But Sweet Little Wolf didn't leap out of bed and chase Red Riding Hood. She hid under the covers and sobbed great big tears.

"I don't want to be a Big Bad Wolf," she cried.

"I want to listen to fairy tales."

Red Riding Hood felt sorry for Sweet Little Wolf.
She told the woodcutter that she was perfectly safe
and wrote a letter in her very best handwriting:

Dear Mr. and Mrs. Wolf,

Once upon a time, there lived
a little wolf that didn't want
to eat girls. She loved all things
pretty and pink, and dreamed of
being a good, kind wolf.
So, this story has a different
ending. A happy ending.

Best wishes,
Red Riding Hood

Dear Mr. and Mrs. Wolf,

Once upon a time, there lived a little wolf that didn't want to eat girls. She loved all things pretty and pink, and dreamed of being a good, kind wolf. So, this story has a different ending. A happy ending.

Best wishes,
Red Riding Hood

☺ friends

wolf. So, this ~~Little~~ has

Sweet Little Wolf ran home with Red Riding Hood's letter. Mr. and Mrs. Wolf were delighted to have their little wolf back. They had been worried, particularly when they heard about the woodcutter from their forest friends.

"It doesn't matter that you aren't a Big Bad Wolf. We love you just the way you are," said Mrs. Wolf, tucking her into bed.

Little Wolf fell fast asleep dreaming of princesses and magical lands and . . .

lovely little girls!
Well, she was a wolf after all!

Once upon
a time . . .